Messier 1985

W9-BPO-796

I'LL FIX ANT

AN ALADDIN BOOK
Atheneum

BY JUDITH VIORST
PICTURES BY ARNOLD LOBEL

PUBLISHED BY ATHENEUM
ALL RIGHTS RESERVED
TEXT COPYRIGHT © 1969 BY JUDITH VIORST
PICTURES COPYRIGHT © 1969 BY ARNOLD LOBEL
ORIGINALLY PUBLISHED BY HARPER AND ROW
(THE TEXT OF *I'll Fix Anthony* WITH SELECTED ILLUSTRATIONS WAS PUBLISHED PREVIOUS
TO THE HARPER EDITION IN *McCall's Magazine*)
PUBLISHED SIMULTANEOUSLY IN CANADA BY MCCLELLAND & STEWART, LTD.
MANUFACTURED IN THE UNITED STATES OF AMERICA BY
CONNECTICUT PRINTERS, INC., BLOOMFIELD, CONNECTICUT
ISBN: 0-689-70761-4
FIRST ALADDIN EDITION.

To my mother and father, the ideal grandparents

My brother
Anthony

can read books now,

but he won't read any books to me.

He plays checkers
with Bruce
from his school.
But when
I want to play
he says Go away or I'll clobber you.

I let him wear
my Snoopy sweat shirt,
but he never lets me
borrow his sword.

Mother says deep down
in his heart Anthony loves me.

Anthony says deep down
in his heart he thinks I stink.

Mother says deep deep down
in his heart,
where he doesn't even know it,
Anthony loves me.

YOU STINK

Anthony says
deep deep down
in his heart he still thinks I stink.

When I'm six

I'll fix Anthony.

When I'm six a dog

will follow me home,

and she'll beg for me and roll over
and lick my face.

If Anthony tries to pet her,
she'll give him a bite.

When I'm six Anthony will have
the German  measles,

and my father will take me
to a baseball game.

Then Anthony will have
 the mumps,

and my mother will take me
to the flower show.

Then Anthony will have a virus,

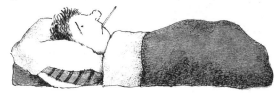

and my grandfather
will take me to the movies.

I won't have to save popcorn
for Anthony unless I want to.

When I'm six we'll have
a skipping contest,
and I'll skip faster.

Then we'll have
a jumping contest,
and I'll jump higher.

Then we'll
do Eeny-Meeny-Miney-Mo,
and Anthony
will be O-U-T.
He'll be very M-A-D.

When I'm six I'll read

Anthony will still
be reading ABC

Who are you voting for, Anthony?
I'll ask him.

When I'm six I'll stand
on my head,
and my legs won't wobble.

Anthony's legs
will wobble a lot.

If someone tickles me,
I'll keep standing
on my head.

If someone pinches me,
I'll keep standing
on my head.

If someone says
Give up
or I'll clobber you,
I'll keep standing on my head.
Anthony will give up at tickles.

When I'm six I'll know
how to  sharpen pencils.

Here's how you do it,
Anthony, I'll say.

When I'm six I'll float,
but Anthony will sink
to the bottom.
I'll dive off the board,
but Anthony will change his mind.

I'll breathe in and out when I should,
but Anthony will only go

GLUG GLUG

When I'm six I'll be tall, and Anthony
will be short because I'll eat things
like carrots and potatoes,
and he'll eat things like
jelly beans and root beer.

I'll put his red sneakers
on the top shelf, and if
he stands on a chair,
he still won't be able
to reach them.

He'll tell me
Get down
my sneakers,
and I'll tell him
Say please,

and if he doesn't say
please, he can't have
his sneakers
for a hundred
years.

When I'm six I'll add 7 and 4 and 10 and 3 inside my mind.

Anthony will just add 1 and 1 and 2, and he'll have to use his fingers.

When I'm six we'll have a race,
and I'll be at the corner when Anthony
hasn't even passed the fireplug.

The next time I'll give him
a head start, but it won't help.

When I'm six friends will call me on the telephone.

No one will call Anthony.

I'll sleep at Charlie's house and Eddie's and Diana's, but Anthony will always sleep at home.

See you later, Anthony, I'll tell him.

When I'm six
I'll help people
carry their groceries
from the supermarket,

and they'll say
My, you're strong.

I don't think
Anthony
will be
strong enough.

When I'm six
I'll be able to tell
left and right,
but Anthony
will be all mixed up.

I'll be
able
to tell time,
but Anthony will be all mixed up.

I'll be able to tell my street and my city
and sometimes my zip code,
but Anthony will be all mixed up.

If he ever gets lost,
I guess I'll have to go find him.

When I'm six Anthony
will still be falling
off his bike.

I'll ride by with   no hands.

Still falling off
that bike?
I'll ask
Anthony.

When I'm six I'll let Dr. Ross look down my throat with a stick.

If he has to give me a shot, I won't even holler.

Try to be brave like your brother, Dr. Ross will tell Anthony.

But Anthony won't.

When I'm six
my teeth 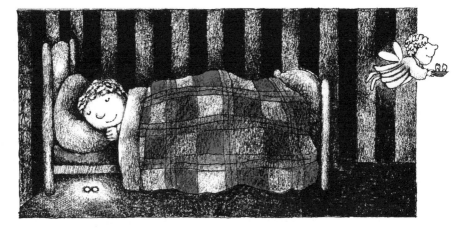 will fall out,

and I'll put them under the bed,
and the tooth fairy will take
them away and leave dimes.

Anthony's teeth won't fall out.

He'll wiggle and wiggle them, but they won't fall out.

I might sell him one of my teeth,

TEETH 25¢

but I might not.

When I'm six I'll go BINGO all the time.
Anthony won't even go BINGO once.

I'll win all the tic-tac-toes if I'm *X*,
and I'll win them all if I'm *O*.
Too bad, Anthony, I'll say.

Anthony is chasing me out
of the playroom.

He says I stink.
He says he is going to clobber me.
I have to run now, but I won't
have to run when I'm six.

When I'm six

I'll fix Anthony.